# DEMETER
## — AND —
# PERSEPHONE

RETOLD BY HUGH LUPTON & DANIEL MORDEN

ILLUSTRATED BY CAROLE HÉNAFF

Barefoot Books
step inside a story

# Contents

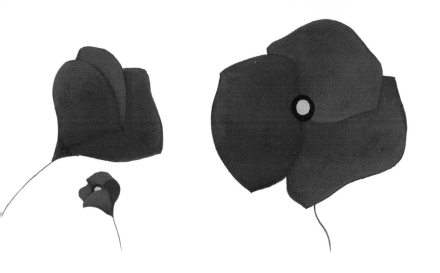

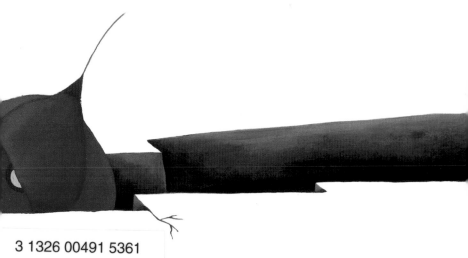

# CHAPTER ONE

# INTO THIN AIR

I MAGINE THREE WORLDS. ONE world is above us. It is perfect, impossible, inhabited by bright immortals. Imagine Mount Olympus. On his throne sits sky god Zeus. He is all-powerful.

He is watching our world below.

Imagine another world, a world under ours. A world without hope or joy.

Mist. Silence. Bitter cold. The Land of the Dead. On his throne sits the lord of darkness, Hades, his eyes as dark and deep as open graves.

7

He is watching our world above.

In between these two worlds, imagine our green Earth, bursting with life, burgeoning growth. The air is heavy with the scent of flowers and the songs of birds. This world is ruled over by Demeter, goddess of the harvest.

Zeus above, Hades below, were watching. They were watching a female figure walking through a meadow.

This was Persephone, the daughter of Demeter. Persephone, that sweet young shoot, shining with youth and life, was gathering flowers with a nymph. She saw a poppy, her favorite flower. She knelt to pick one —

The ground cracked. The earth and air shook. A gaping gash appeared. It belched bitter, acrid fog. Behind them they could hear a deafening thunder. They looked over their

shoulders and stumbled at the sight. Hades!
The grim king himself, in a chariot drawn
by four Night Mares, burst forth from the
Underworld! He cracked his whip. His horses

hurtled towards them. Persephone and the nymph lifted up their skirts to flee. But already the king of terrors was towering over them. Hades leaned over the side of his chariot and plucked Persephone from the earth.

She called her mother's name, but there was no answer. The nymph flung out her hands and grasped Persephone's dress. The dress tore, and then the chariot was gone. It had plunged into the darkness below. The gash in the earth closed to a scar. The nymph was alone.

As she plunged into the gloom, Persephone kept calling her mother's name. But no one came to her call. Demeter was far away.

The nymph was beside herself. She cast about helplessly. She sank to her knees. At her feet were the flowers that Persephone had picked moments before: soft crocuses, bright irises, hyacinth, rosebuds and lilies, dying in the dirt. She tried to gather them, but they tumbled from her trembling hands. She wept. So profound was her grief that she melted into sorrow. Every pore of her body wept tears, until all that was left of her was a torn dress floating in a salty pool.

Demeter, the goddess of growth, the bringer of life, of the crown of corn, of the lustrous hair, whom we must thank for every full mouth and every bulging belly. Demeter, far above on Mount Olympus, caught a snatch of sound. She was pierced with fear. She called her daughter's name: there came no reply. She descended to the earth. She searched the world. Neither Eos, goddess of the dawn, nor Hesperus, the evening star, found her resting. As she passed by, the flowers wilted. Anguish aged her. Her crown of corn fell from her brow.

Her lustrous hair turned dirty gray. Her radiant robes were ripped to rags.

For nine days, for nine nights, with a flaming torch in each hand, she searched the earth. The wind moaned. The sky cried. Once in the early morning a shepherd saw her searching, her face a mask of anguish, marked with shadow and fire. She was a pitiful sight. He turned away and uttered a prayer.

# CHAPTER TWO

# THE STRANGE GUEST

O NE DAY, BROKEN, SOBBING, Demeter sat by a well.

Nearby the well there was a cottage. In the cottage lived an old woman, her daughter and the daughter's child, a baby boy.

The grandmother saw this stranger sitting by the well. She saw the fine clothes ripped to rags. Beneath the filth the stranger was beautiful.

The grandmother drew water from the well with a bronze pitcher. She offered some to the stranger. The stranger sipped. She

scraped the tears from her cheeks with the heel of her hand.

"Come out of the wind and the rain. Come with me now," said the grandmother. She took the stranger's hand in her own. Silently, the stranger stood. She let herself be led into the cottage.

The baby was crying. He'd been crying all morning. The sight of the stranger silenced him. He stretched out his scrawny arms.

"Look at that!" said the grandmother. "Daughter, give him to her!"

The daughter looked dubiously at the filthy visitor. The grandmother smiled and urged her, "Go on!"

She handed the child to the stranger. The baby smiled and cooed. He opened his little hands. The grandmother laughed. "You have the touch!"

That night the stranger stayed with them. She said little and ate nothing. But they could see the presence of the child brought her comfort. And the baby was happy, serene.

# CHAPTER THREE

# THE PROMISE

THE NEXT MORNING THE BABY looked for the stranger. The mother was exhausted, and there seemed no harm in this woman, so she passed him over. The stranger took the child gratefully. She cradled him. For a moment she looked up and smiled. The mother was taken aback. Never had she seen such a stare! Her eyes were golden, like the sun.

The mother said, "Have you any children?"

"I have a daughter," said the stranger.

"Is she married?" asked the mother.

Tears spattered onto the baby's face.

"She is gone."

The mother was suddenly filled with pity. "Why don't you stay with us? You could look after my son. We'd be glad of your help," she offered.

"I will tend to him at night. You sleep in the bedroom. I'll care for him here," said the stranger.

"A few nights' sleep would be a blessing!" the mother said.

The stranger said, "Then don't come through at night. Don't even look. Stay in there, no matter what you hear. Do you promise?"

That stare again . . .

"I promise."

"No harm will come to the child," the stranger promised.

The days turned to weeks; the weeks turned to months. The stranger stayed with them. Mostly she was silent, mute with grief.

The baby thrived. The mother and the grandmother marveled. He had been a whining runt. Now he was chubby, healthy, happy. He was so beautiful... like a god.

One night, in her bedroom, the mother was woken by the sound of her son chuckling in the room beyond. Curious, she crept to the door. She opened it a crack.

The stranger was holding the baby by his ankle, dangling him in the flames of the fire. He wriggled and giggled, and as the flames tickled his arms, his back, his chest, the mother screamed.

"What are you doing?"

The stranger looked up. She lifted the baby from the fire and laid him carefully on the flagstones. She said, "If only you had kept your promise. I was burning away his mortality. He would never have died. He would have cheated

the three Fates. But now he'll grow old and wither, like the rest of you."

She strode into the dark.

# CHAPTER FOUR

# THE TRUTH COMES OUT

THE NEXT NIGHT, IN THE village of Eleusis, there was a feast. A strange woman came out of the darkness to watch the dancing and revelry. A cluster of farmworkers, drinking by the fire, noticed her and stared. She stared back. They looked away.

"Hey! Swineherd!" said one. "Tell that story again!"

"What story?" said the swineherd.

"Of who you saw," another one said.

The men laughed. The swineherd frowned and said, "How many times have I told you? It was Hades! It was! First there were two maidens gathering flowers. Pretty things they were; eyes like buds. Then this crack appeared in the ground. Hades came out in his chariot! He grabbed one of them and took her under!"

The men hooted with laughter. But in an instant the stranger had grabbed the swineherd's arm, her golden eyes fixed on him.

"Tell me where."

He told her all that he knew.

Demeter flew to the place. She found the scar in the earth and beside it a salty pool.

The nymph wanted to speak. She wanted to tell the terrible news about Persephone, but her lips, her tongue, her mouth were just water now. So with her shifting currents she summoned the torn dress.

Demeter knew it at once. She sank to her knees. The grass around her wilted and died. The trees wept their leaves. The corn in the fields withered and shriveled in the husk. The apples, the figs, rotted as they grew. The ground cracked and crumbled. Clouds of dust blotted out the eye of the sun. Everywhere there was want, hunger, suffering, famine, death. Desperate, men became no better than beasts. Children throttled their parents for a crust.

News spread. Demeter walked the earth, searching for her child. The people made temples and altars to her. They gave her whatever scant offerings they could find. They begged her to show them mercy, entreating her to give life back to the land. But she heard only the distant cry of her child, the cry that had first summoned her from the sky.

<br />

CHAPTER FIVE

# ZEUS STEPS IN

UP ON MOUNT OLYMPUS, Zeus shuddered. The earth was screaming. This was not in his plan. He sent the messenger of the gods, Hermes, to fetch Demeter. Hermes commanded her in the name of Zeus to accompany him. But it was as though she'd been turned to stone. The only signs of life were the tears carving grooves in her cheeks. Silver-tongued Hermes tried to persuade her. His words could charm the wings from the back of a bird, but not even he could move her.

Zeus sent every god and goddess to Demeter offering gifts, to beg, wheedle and cajole her.

Eventually Zeus had to descend from the heavens himself. For him, she turned her head: "You gave my child to the god of death. Since he has her for a wife, let him have the earth for a dowry. This world will be his. Let it be as dark and desolate as his realm."

"Your daughter is a queen," Zeus said. "She sits beside the king of shadows. You should be proud of her."

"Persephone does not belong below. She loves the warmth of the sun on her skin. She loves birdsong. Down there she hears only the moans of the dead," said Demeter.

Zeus looked about. He heard no prayers in his honor, only screams and suffering. The only burnt offering that rose into the sky was the smoke of funeral pyres.

"You know the laws. There are forces to which even I must answer. The three Fates have decreed: Persephone will be freed...provided she has not tasted Hades's food."

CHAPTER SIX

# THE COMPROMISE

So HERMES DESCENDED TO the Land of the Dead. As he traveled across the plain he saw poppies growing, each like a shimmering drop of blood. He followed their trail to the hall of the grim king.

"Mighty Zeus has decreed: Persephone must be freed, unless she has tasted your food," said wing-heeled Hermes.

Something flickered in the caves of Hades's eyes. He bowed his head.

"Very well."

Persephone returned to the earth. When Demeter saw her daughter, her heart opened like a flower. The soil grew long ears of corn like waving hair, the whole wide Earth was fragrant with blooms and blossom. She stretched out her hands. Persephone reached for her mother, but Demeter saw on her daughter's palm a stain as red as blood.

"What is that mark?" she asked Persephone.

"Only the juice of a pomegranate."

"Did you eat?"

Persephone looked at her mother. "Six seeds," she said.

In the darkness below, the king of terrors grinned.

Demeter returned to Zeus.

"I have been tricked again! Imagine a world where nothing green grows, a world without hope or joy, where no birds sing, where night

31

blots out the eye of day. This is not the Land of the Dead that I describe," said Demeter. "This will be the Land of the Living, unless you give me back my daughter."

Zeus found a compromise.

Ever since then, for six months of the year — six months for six seeds — Persephone lives with her husband in the Land of the Dead. The moment she departs, her mother Demeter's heart turns cold with grief, so our world is silent, dark and desolate.

And for six months Persephone lives here on the earth with her mother. The moment she returns, Demeter is filled with joy, and from the earth comes new life, budding, burgeoning growth. There is light, warmth, birdsong.

After Zeus's judgement, Demeter returned to the people of Eleusis, the people who had looked after her in her anguish. She taught

them the rituals they must observe to welcome Persephone back to the world, rituals that would ensure that their harvests would always be plentiful.

So it was and so it is.

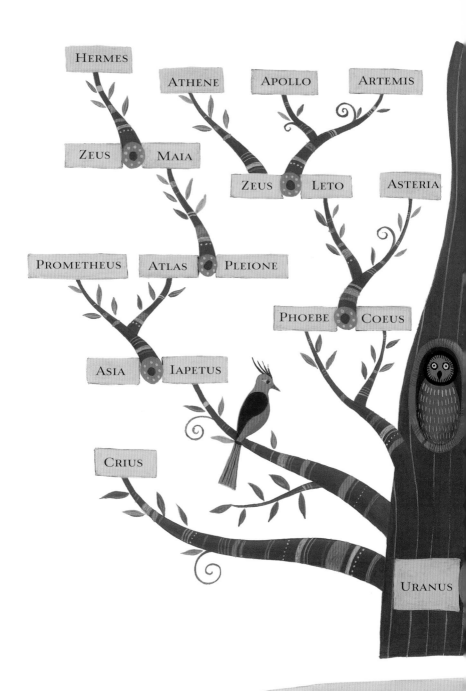

HERMES

ATHENE

APOLLO

ARTEMIS

ZEUS    MAIA

ZEUS    LETO

ASTERIA

PROMETHEUS    ATLAS    PLEIONE

PHOEBE    COEUS

ASIA    IAPETUS

CRIUS

URANUS

FAMILY TREE C

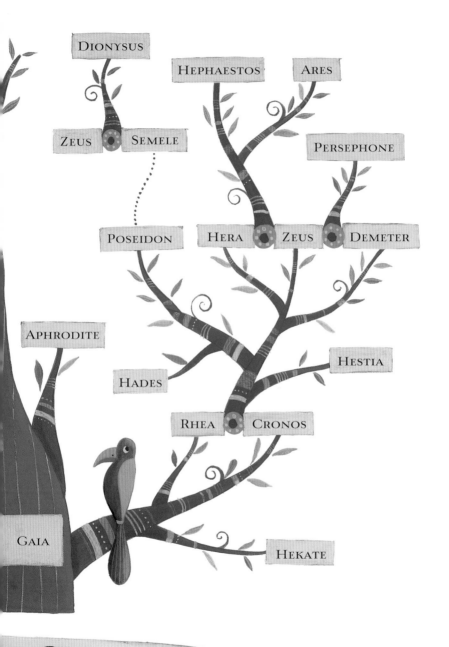

DIONYSUS

ZEUS   SEMELE

HEPHAESTOS   ARES

PERSEPHONE

POSEIDON   HERA   ZEUS   DEMETER

APHRODITE

HADES   HESTIA

RHEA   CRONOS

GAIA

HEKATE

ΗE GREEK GODS

## ZEUS
### GOD OF THUNDER

## HERA
### GODDESS OF MARRIA

## APHRODITE
### GODDESS OF LOVE

## POSEIDON
### GOD OF THE SEA

## APOLLO
### GOD OF THE SUN

## ATHENE
### GODDESS OF WISDO

**DIONYSUS**
GOD OF WINE

**ARTEMIS**
GODDESS OF THE HUNT

**DEMETER**
DESS OF THE HARVEST

**ARES**
GOD OF WAR

**HEPHAESTOS**
GOD OF FIRE

**HERMES**
MESSENGER GOD

# Demeter
## — and —
# Persephone

To Mary, Margaret, Marion, Liz,
Rowan and Alice — H. L. and D. M.

To Grace and her twin sisters,
Olivia and Camille — C. H.

• • • • • • • • •

## Pronunciation guide

Demeter . . . . . . . . . . Dem-EET-er
Eleusis . . . . . . . . . . . . el-EE-yoo-sis
Eos . . . . . . . . . . . . . . . EE-yoss
Fates . . . . . . . . . . . . . FAYTZ
Hades . . . . . . . . . . . . HAY-deez
Hermes . . . . . . . . . . HER-meez
Hesperus . . . . . . . . . HESS-per-us

Mount Olympus . . . . MOUNT oh-LIM-pus
nymph . . . . . . . . . . . . NIMF
Persephone . . . . . . . . per-SEH-fon-ee
pomegranate . . . . . . . POM-eh-gran-et
pyre . . . . . . . . . . . . . . PIE-er
Zeus . . . . . . . . . . . . . . ZYOOSE

• • • • • • • • •

## Bibliography

Garfield, Leon and Edward Blishen. *The God Beneath the Sea*. Illustrated by Charles Keeping.
    London: Corgi, 1973.
Graves, Robert. *The Greek Myths*. London: Pelican Books, 1955.
*The Homeric Hymns*. Translated by Jules Cashford. London: Penguin, 2003.
Kerényi, Carl. *Eleusis: Archetypal Image of Mother and Daughter*. Bollingen Series. Princeton, NJ:
    Princeton University Press, 1967.

• • • • • • • • •

Barefoot Books
2067 Massachusetts Ave
Cambridge, MA 02140

Text copyright © 2013 by Hugh Lupton
    and Daniel Morden
Illustrations copyright © 2013 by Carole Hénaff
The moral rights of Hugh Lupton, Daniel
    Morden and Carole Hénaff have been asserted

First published in the United States of America
    by Barefoot Books, Inc in 2013
All rights reserved

Graphic design by Ryan Scheife,
    Mayfly Design, Minneapolis, MN
Color separation by B & P International,
    Hong Kong
Printed in China on 100% acid-free paper
This book was typeset in Agamemnon, Dante
    MT Std and Mynaruse
The illustrations were prepared in acrylics

ISBN 978-1-84686-834-4

Library of Congress Cataloging-in-Publication
    Data is available under LCCN 2012020208

1  3  5  7  9  8  6  4  2